THE HULK RULES!

adapted by Orli Zuravicky
based on the screenplay by Zak Penn and Edward Norton
illustrated by The Artifact Group

SIMON SPOTLIGHT
New York   London   Toronto   Sydney

SIMON SPOTLIGHT
An imprint of Simon & Schuster Children's Publishing Division
1230 Avenue of the Americas, New York, New York 10020
SIMON SPOTLIGHT and colophon are registered trademarks of Simon & Schuster, Inc.
Manufactured in the United States of America
First Edition   10 9 8 7 6 5 4 3 2 1
ISBN-13: 978-1-4169-6054-6
ISBN-10: 1-4169-6054-6

It was a sunny day in Porto Verde, Brazil, and Bruce Banner was on his morning run. He checked his pulse monitor: ninety beats per minute. Good, he thought—as long as I can keep it this way.

For five years Bruce had been living in hiding. He vowed to stay hidden until he found a cure for his condition. See, when Bruce Banner got angry, and his heart rate got too high, he transformed into an enormous, green, out-of-control monster—a monster known as The Hulk.

Later that night, Bruce experimented with the serum that a fellow scientist, Mr. Blue, had written him about. Bruce mixed the serum with a sample of his blood and watched. But nothing happened.

Bruce thought about why he had left home in the first place—how he became The Hulk and had almost killed Betty Ross, another scientist and the love of his life. Never again, he thought.

The next morning Bruce mailed his sample to Mr. Blue.

A few days later, Bruce received good news: Mr. Blue had figured out a way to lessen the gamma saturation in Bruce's blood. And in order to come up with the right formula, Mr. Blue needed to know more about Bruce's first exposure to gamma radiation.

Easy enough, Bruce thought. All he had to do was go back to his old lab at Culver University to get the results of his experiment.

The U. S. military had been searching for Bruce since his disappearance, and they finally had a lead—a possible case of gamma sickness in Milwaukee. The cause was a guarana soda bottled in Porto Verde, Brazil. Major Kathleen Sparr immediately told General Ross about it.

"Get the Agency people looking for a white man at that bottling plant," General Ross commanded. "Tell them not to contact him—or he'll run!"

A few days later, General Ross and Major Sparr set off for Brazil with a team of special forces. The mission was headed by Captain Emil Blonsky, a Purple Heart soldier.

"This is your target and location," Major Sparr told the team, holding up a picture of Bruce Banner. "He's a fugitive from the U.S. government, and he's dangerous. Don't wait to see if he's a fighter."

That night Captain Blonsky's Special Forces team arrived at Porto Verde. The soldiers quietly made their way up the stairs to Bruce's apartment.

Boom! Bruce's front door burst off its hinges as they charged inside. A large heap under the bedcovers seemed to indicate that Bruce was sleeping peacefully, but when the captain yanked back the covers, all he found was a mass of pillows and a plastic head.

"Target is on the move!" Captain Blonsky called out.

Bruce ran as fast as he could. He tried to keep his heart rate low, but it wasn't easy. He ducked into the soda bottling plant, but they followed him inside. After a while, he couldn't stop his pulse from rising. He couldn't help turning into The Hulk—and thankfully, becoming The Hulk helped him to escape.

Later, even when he returned to being Bruce Banner, he continued to run as far away as possible.

Shocked by what he had just seen, Captain Blonsky told General Ross, "We didn't lose him; we had him and something hit us. Something big—ten feet tall and green."

"That *was* Banner," Ross replied matter-of-factly.

The general told him that years ago, Bruce Banner had injected himself with gamma radiation during a military experiment. But something went wrong, and it caused Bruce to turn into The Hulk.

I wouldn't mind a little extra strength, Captain Blonsky thought. I can finally be the unbeatable soldier I've always wanted to be. Maybe General Ross can help me out . . .

Later that evening, the general led Captain Blonsky to one of the army's medical labs. "We're going to give you a very low dose of the Super Soldier Serum," General Ross said. "At the first sign of a side effect, we'll stop."

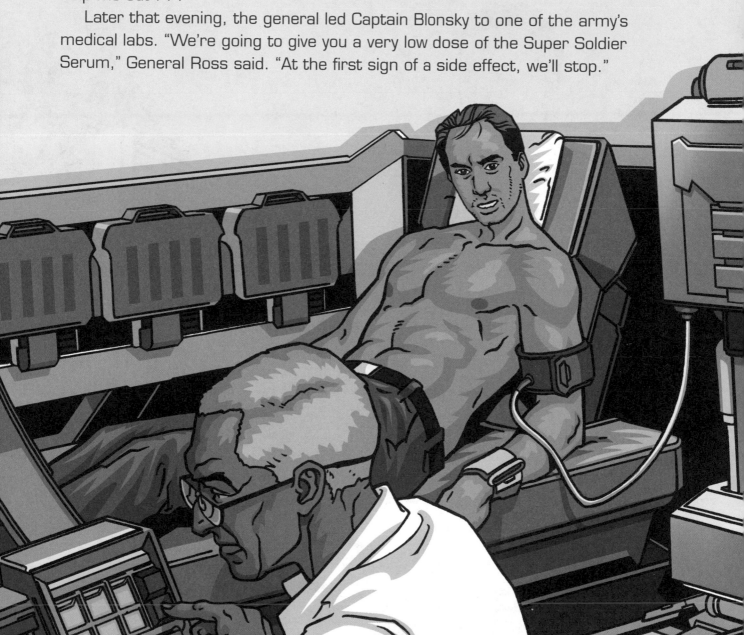

Back in the United States, Bruce headed for the lab at Culver University, where he had infected himself and The Hulk was born.

Bruce found a computer terminal and managed to access the school's network after a few tries. He quickly searched for the original data.

USMD Research Protocol 456-72375: No Results

Gamma Pulse: No Results

All the data had been erased! It was as if Bruce had never been there . . . as if his experiments had never happened.

Bruce didn't know what to do next, so it was fortunate that he ran into his old friend Betty Ross.

He filled Betty in on Mr. Blue, and the possible cure for his condition. Betty knew that Bruce was talking about Dr. Samuel Sterns.

"He needs the original data for the experiment, but it's gone," Bruce told her. Then Betty surprised Bruce by handing him a card containing the data from his first exposure. "I got it out before they carted it all away," she said.

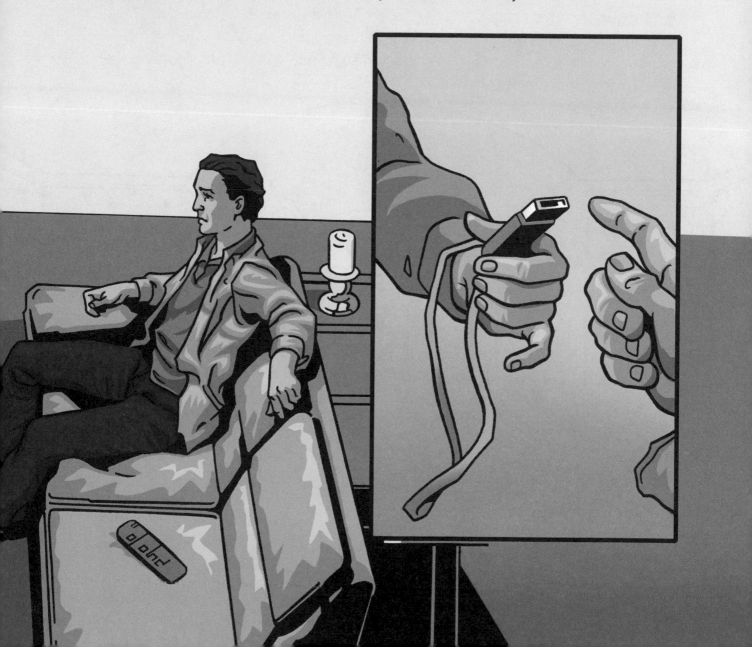

Betty was walking Bruce to the bus station when a sudden thundering noise came from above. Bruce looked to see soldiers coming toward them from all directions. He took off in full sprint and ran through an underpass—only to be stopped by an explosion. As the tunnel filled with smoke, Bruce saw Betty running toward him, and then a soldier grabbing her arm.

That was all it took for Bruce's heart rate to rise. An uncontrollable anger burned inside him, and, once again, The Hulk was set free.

The Hulk continued to grow, ten-feet tall and huge. The soldiers had never seen anything like him. Even Captain Blonsky and his Super Soldier Serum were no match for this monster. The Hulk put up a good fight, and the soldiers finally backed down. Once again, The Hulk managed to escape—and this time he took Betty with him.

Betty and The Hulk sought shelter in a cave somewhere in the forest. Even as The Hulk, he seemed to recognize who she was and knew that he had to protect her. After a while, when Bruce's heart rate returned to normal, he told Betty, "It's time to go find Mr. Blue."

They headed for Empire State University in New York City. On the way, Bruce sent Mr. Blue the original data from Betty's memory chip. He hoped with all his heart that with it, Mr. Blue could find a cure.

Captain Blonksy was hurt pretty badly in his fight with The Hulk, and doctors had even told him he would never walk again. But it was not long before Emil Blonsky was fully healed—and determined not to let The Hulk defeat him once more.

I need something stronger, the soldier thought.

A few days later, Captain Blonsky received his second injection of the Super Soldier Serum.

Bruce and Betty found Dr. Sterns in the lab at Empire State University. He told them that he had created an antidote, but Bruce would have to turn into The Hulk to test it.

Without stopping to think about it, Bruce raised his heart rate, and became The Hulk. Dr. Sterns immediately injected him with the special antidote. And in minutes—to everyone's amazement—it worked! Bruce was himself again.

"You're all right!" Betty cried. "It's over!"

Just then, Captain Blonsky and his team came smashing through the lab window. A split second later, a tranquilizer dart landed on Bruce's neck, and he collapsed at once.

As Bruce was taken to General Ross, Captain Blonsky told Dr. Sterns, "I want what you got out of Banner—or else!"

Frightened, Dr. Sterns injected Blonsky with a sample of Bruce's blood. I'll be the strongest fighter in the world, Captain Blonsky thought. And I will beat The Hulk this time.

Just when General Ross thought he had finally caught the monster, a huge explosion erupted nearby.

"The Hulk's in the street!" a soldier cried over the radio.

Impossible, the general thought. Banner's here with me! Then, right there on his TV screen, General Ross saw a huge, heavily muscled green creature stomping down the city street. It's Blonsky, he realized, a new monster I helped to create.

S&SN **BREAKING NEWS**

CITY IN CHAOS ! MONSTER WRECKS HAVOC ! CI

Bruce was just as alarmed by this new creature, now known as The Abomination. "I'm the only thing that can stop it," he told General Ross.

The Abomination was destroying everything in its path—until it met The Hulk. Every strike The Hulk threw, The Abomination countered with more strength.

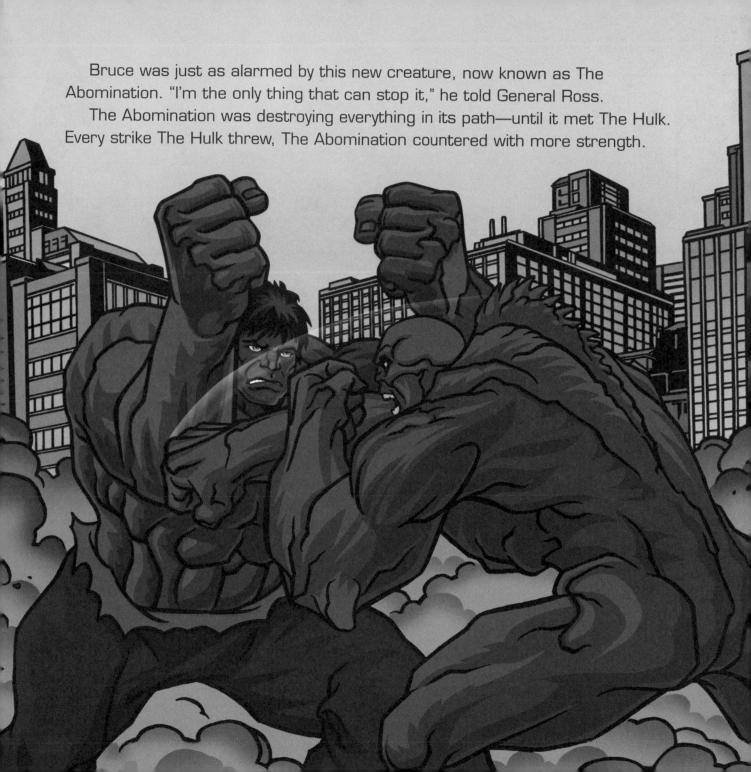

Finally, The Hulk delivered a fateful blow and The Abomination was defeated.

No doubt about it, The Hulk rules!